The Big Performance Collection

Angelina™
Ballerina

Published by Pleasant Company Publications
Based on the text by Katharine Holabird and the illustrations by Helen Craig
From the scripts by Laura Beaumont, Sally Lever, James Mason, Jan Page, and Barbara Slade

Visit our Web site at www.americangirl.com and
Angelina's very own site at www.angelinaballerina.com.

Printed in China

05 06 07 08 09 10 11 C&C 10 9 8 7 6 5 4 3 2 1

Cataloging-in-Publication data available from the Library of Congress

The Big Performance Collection

Based on the classic picture books by Katharine Holabird and Helen Craig

PLEASANT COMPANY PUBLICATIONS™

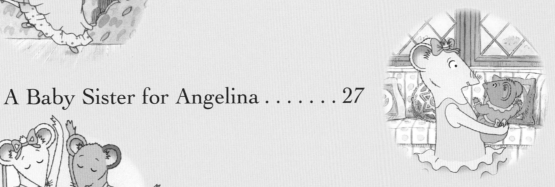

The Royal Banquet

From the script by Sally Lever

Based on the classic picture books
by Katharine Holabird and Helen Craig

Angelina and her family were sitting around the kitchen table, listening to Dr. Tuttle describe the hot-air balloon ride he would soon be taking. "I leave on Saturday morning," he declared.

"You'll be able to see for miles from up there!" said Mr. Mouseling.

"I wish I could go in a hot-air balloon," Angelina added wistfully.

Her daydream was interrupted by a knock at the door. Miss Lilly swept into the kitchen. "I have the most wonderful news!" she exclaimed. "Angelina has been chosen to dance for Queen Seraphina at the Royal Banquet!"

Angelina tried to focus on packing, but she was too excited.
She practiced the moment when she would meet the queen.
"Thank you for having me, Your Highness," said Angelina,
bowing her head.

When Angelina glanced up, she saw her mother—not the queen—standing in the doorway.

"You're supposed to be getting ready!" Mrs. Mouseling scolded playfully. She held up a shimmering dress with tiny blue stars.

Angelina gasped. "It's the most beautiful dress I've ever seen!" she cried, throwing her arms around her mother's waist. Wearing the splendid dress, Angelina would truly be ready to meet the queen.

On the train, Miss Lilly told Angelina stories about growing up with the queen. "When we were your age, we played Tip-Toe-Tumbly. We danced up hillsides on tiptoe, and we tumbled all the way down," said Miss Lilly, her eyes sparkling.

Angelina tried to imagine the queen rolling through grass and mud. Tip-Toe-Tumbly didn't seem like a very royal thing to do!

A waiter pushing a cart of drinks stopped beside Angelina. "We'll take two hot chocolates," said Miss Lilly. But suddenly, the train screeched to a halt. Something was terribly wrong!

"Trains should not break down," Miss Lilly grumbled as she lugged her suitcase across a grassy field. "Especially when we have an appointment at the palace!"

Angelina followed with her own heavy suitcase. "Do you know the way, Miss Lilly?" she asked.

"One field is like any field," replied Miss Lilly. "Each has a gate that leads to a road. This way!"

But the grassy field led to a cornfield, and the stalks were as high as Angelina's shoulders. She craned her neck to see beyond the field. She saw nothing but row after row of golden corn.

At last, Angelina and Miss Lilly reached a gate. "Aha!" exclaimed
Miss Lilly. "What did I tell you!"

Angelina climbed the gate to see what was on the other side. Another
rolling field stretched out before them. Angelina swallowed hard.
"Do you think we're lost?" she asked.

Miss Lilly pushed open the gate and walked on. "Of course not!" she declared. "Keep going, Angelina. Keep going." But after a few steps, Miss Lilly slid down a muddy slope and landed with a *splash!* in the river below.

A short while later, Angelina and a very wet Miss Lilly sat side-by-side in the back of a small fishing boat.

Mr. Scampi, the fisherman, was delighted to have two "royal" guests on board. "The palace is just over the river," he reassured them.

But Mr. Scampi was so busy talking to his guests that he didn't keep an eye on the river ahead. "Watch out!" Angelina and Miss Lilly cried together as the boat crashed straight into a small island.

Now Angelina was sure they would never get to the palace on time. Then Mr. Scampi had one last idea. "A friend lives nearby," he said. "He has a motorcycle, and I'm sure he'd lend it to you."

A motorcycle? Angelina's stomach lurched. Did Miss Lilly know how to drive a motorcycle?

Soon Angelina and Miss Lilly were zooming down a country lane.
Angelina struggled to hold her map steady in the rushing wind.
She called out directions to Miss Lilly: "Left at the gate!"

Miss Lilly could barely hear over the sputter of the engine. "What?" she shouted, and then, "Oh, the gate!" She veered sharply left. The motorcycle bounced through a row of bushes and toppled over, tossing Angelina onto the ground.

"Miss Lilly!" Angelina cried. "Where are you?"

"Don't worry," Miss Lilly said weakly. She crawled out of the bushes and pried the helmet from her head. "I'm fine, darling."

Angelina and Miss Lilly had survived the crash, but Angelina's packed suitcase had not. Her dress, torn and muddied, lay sprawled on the ground.

"Oh, no!" Angelina cried as she gathered the remains of the dress. The tears that she had been holding back began to fall. "My b-beautiful dress," she sobbed.

"Please don't cry," said Miss Lilly, kneeling beside Angelina. "Sometimes things don't turn out the way they were planned."

Then, from up above, Angelina and Miss Lilly heard a familiar voice calling to them…

"Hello, Miss Lilly! Need a lift?"

Angelina and Miss Lilly glanced upward and were astonished to see a hot-air balloon drifting toward them. It was Dr. Tuttle!

The balloon landed on the ground with a *thud*. Dr. Tuttle helped Angelina and Miss Lilly into the basket, and soon they were floating across the beautiful blue sky toward the palace.

"You're an angel, Dr. Tuttle," Miss Lilly said dramatically. Angelina felt like an angel, too, flying high above the ground.

19

When the balloon reached the palace, a footman helped Miss Lilly, Angelina, and Dr. Tuttle out of the basket.

Queen Seraphina was waiting for them, and by her side was Princess Valentine, who looked as if she was just Angelina's age. Miss Lilly introduced the two mouselings to each other with a wave of her paw. "This is my beautiful little star, Angelina," she said to the princess.

"Gosh!" exclaimed Princess Valentine as she looked Angelina up and down. "Have you been playing Tip-Toe-Tumbly?"

Angelina suddenly remembered how muddy and rumpled she looked. "Oh, no!" she cried. "How can I dance at the Royal Banquet like this?"

"Don't worry, Angelina," said the princess. "Come with me."

When the stage curtains opened at the Royal Banquet, Angelina was dressed like a princess from head to toe. She wore a twinkling tiara and a beautiful gown that swirled as she danced.

Sitting high above the stage, Miss Lilly was dressed like royalty, too. She dabbed away tears of pride as she watched Angelina strike her final pose. The audience broke into applause.

"Angelina is a real star," Queen Seraphina declared to Miss Lilly. "Just like you, my dear. Just like you."

When the hot-air balloon set off for home the next morning, Angelina was still dreaming of dancing at the Royal Banquet and of the journey that had brought her there. "That was the best time ever in my whole life!" Angelina exclaimed.

Miss Lilly laughed and patted Angelina's shoulder. "You see, my darling," she said, "things don't always turn out as you think they will."

"You're right!" Angelina agreed as the balloon drifted into the sunset. "Sometimes they turn out even *better*."

A Baby Sister for Angelina

From the script by Jan Page

Based on the classic picture books
by Katharine Holabird and Helen Craig

The end-of-year show had finally arrived, and Miss Lilly's ballet students were practicing their steps one last time.

Angelina was especially excited, because her family was expecting a new baby. Soon Angelina would be a big sister!

"One, two, three…" Miss Lilly counted. "Good, Angelina!"
Just then, the telephone rang.

"You're sure to win Miss Lilly's special prize tonight, Angelina,"
said William as Miss Lilly rushed off to answer the telephone.

When Miss Lilly returned, she had wonderful news: "Angelina,
the baby has arrived!"

Angelina twirled with excitement all the way home. She burst through the bedroom door, where she found her mother cuddling the tiniest mouseling Angelina had ever seen.

"We're calling her Polly," said Mrs. Mouseling.

Angelina's heart leaped. "Oh, a baby sister!" she exclaimed. Angelina thought of all the wonderful things she could teach little Polly. "I can bring her to ballet lessons," she said.

Mrs. Mouseling laughed tenderly. "Not quite yet," she said. "But would you like to hold her?"

That evening, just after dinner, the doorbell rang. Angelina was surprised to see her best friend, Alice, and her mother on the doorstep. "Come along, Angelina," said Mrs. Nimbletoes. "We're going to be late for the performance!"

Angelina's face fell. "Aren't you coming?" she asked her father.

"I need to look after your mother and the baby," he said gently.

Angelina felt sad and confused. Her parents *always* came to the end-of-year show. Would everything change now that Polly was here?

Angelina's heart was heavy as she danced. She checked the audience again and again, hoping her parents had changed their minds and had come to watch her dance.

When the performance ended, Miss Lilly stepped forward holding a beautiful china doll. "And now, it's time to present my award to the Most Promising Dancer of the Year," Miss Lilly announced. "Angelina Mouseling!"

But Angelina was still searching the crowd and scarcely heard Miss Lilly's words.

"Angelina," Miss Lilly said again. She handed Angelina the doll. "What a happy day this is for you, dear," said Miss Lilly.

Angelina tried to smile, but hot tears burned her eyes. *It would have been,* she thought, *if only they had come.*

The next morning, Angelina brought the china doll to show her mother. But Mrs. Mouseling was busy with Polly. "Angelina, can you watch the baby for a few minutes?" she asked.

Angelina sighed and plopped down onto the bed. Polly smiled up at her, and Angelina's heart softened.

"See this?" said Angelina, setting the china doll beside Polly. "I won it for being the Most Promising Dancer of the Year."

Polly cooed and reached for the doll with her tiny paw. The doll rolled over once, twice, and then . . .

Crash! The doll fell to the floor.

"Oh, Polly, how could you!" Angelina cried as she dropped to her knees and gathered up the broken pieces of her beautiful doll.

Polly, frightened by the sound of breaking china, began to wail. When Mrs. Mouseling hurried in, she found both of her daughters in tears.

"There, there, Polly, it's all right," said Mrs. Mouseling as she scooped up the baby and carried her out of the room.

Angelina felt miserable. "Polly, Polly, Polly!" she called after her mother. "You don't care about me at all anymore!"

Angelina stomped down the hall to her room. She packed her
favorite things in a suitcase and lugged it down the stairs.
"I'm going to Grandma and Grandpa's!" she muttered angrily.

But no one heard her over Polly's cries, and Angelina made it out
the door and all the way down to the bus stop.

When the bus arrived, Angelina picked up her suitcase. The doors
of the bus opened, and there stood Grandma and Grandpa!

Angelina threw her arms around Grandma's neck. "I'm coming to
live with you!" cried Angelina.

"What?" said Grandma, surprised. "Don't be silly, Angelina," she said, patting Angelina's back. "Your Mum and Dad need you to help look after the baby! I'll bet they're wondering where you are right now."

Grandpa carried Angelina's suitcase all the way home, and Angelina told her grandparents about the prize she had won at ballet. When they reached the house, Angelina felt much better.

"I'll show you my prize now, Grandpa," Angelina chattered as they stepped through the front door. "Maybe you can glue her back together."

But Grandpa and Grandma were already hurrying off into the living room. "Not now, dear," called Grandpa. "First we have to see the baby!"

Angelina was shocked. Even Grandma and Grandpa cared more about the baby than they did about her! Angelina whirled around and raced up the stairs. She slammed her bedroom door. She threw her toys across the room, one after another. "I changed my mind," she cried. "I don't want a baby sister!"

From downstairs, Angelina's parents and grandparents could hear the *thumps* and *bumps* coming from Angelina's bedroom. "Whatever is going on?" asked Grandma.

"Oh, dear," said Mrs. Mouseling as she hurried up the stairs.

She found Angelina lying facedown on her bed, sobbing. Mrs. Mouseling rushed to the bed and pulled Angelina into her arms.

"Y-you don't care about me anymore!" wailed Angelina.

"Of course I do," said her mother, rocking her from side to side.
"I love you just as much as ever. *You* were my very first baby."

Mrs. Mouseling wiped away Angelina's tears and led her downstairs.

"Come and have a cuddle," said Mr. Mouseling. He lifted Angelina into his arms.

"You know, we were so sad to miss Angelina's performance last night," said Mrs. Mouseling to Angelina's grandparents. "I wonder if she will dance for us now."

"Yes, you must, Angelina!" said her grandparents.

Mr. Mouseling set Angelina down and picked up his fiddle. He began to play for her.

Angelina took a few shy steps and then let the music carry her away. She twirled and leaped around the living room floor.

Polly giggled as she watched Angelina dance. "She wants to dance with you!" said Mrs. Mouseling. She held Polly out toward Angelina.

"Really?" said Angelina. She cradled Polly in her arms and gently swayed with her, back and forth. Polly squealed with delight, and Angelina smiled. *This* was just how she had imagined it would feel to be a big sister.

The next morning, Angelina found her mother cooking break-
fast and her father reading the paper. Everything seemed back
to normal—except, of course, that baby Polly was sitting at the
table, too. When she saw Angelina, Polly held out her arms.

"I'll take her," said Angelina. She snuggled into a chair with her baby sister and began bouncing her on her knee. Polly giggled.

"You know, Polly," Angelina began, "as soon as you can walk, I'm going to teach you your first ballet steps. And then we'll buy you some ballet shoes. And then I'll take you to Miss Lilly's."

Polly cooed, as if she understood every word. Angelina hugged her close and whispered, "You know, Polly, you really are the Most Promising Baby Sister of the Year."

Angelina's Dance of Friendship

From the script by James Mason

BASED ON THE CLASSIC PICTURE BOOKS
BY KATHARINE HOLABIRD AND HELEN CRAIG

"Well done, my darlings!" exclaimed Miss Lilly at the end of ballet class. "Now, before you go, I have some news."

The mouselings gathered around Miss Lilly.

"I am sure you remember Anya Moussorsky, who visited us from Dacovia last year," said Miss Lilly. "Anya is coming to Chipping Cheddar this summer to learn ballet."

"Oh, Alice!" Angelina squealed as she grabbed her best friend's paws and spun her in a circle. "Isn't that wonderful?"

That evening, Angelina pleaded with her mother to let Anya stay at their house for the summer. "Please, Mum," said Angelina. "She won't be any trouble!"

"Of course she won't," said Mrs. Mouseling. "But where will she sleep?"

"In my room," Angelina chattered. "Dad will move another bed in, won't you, Dad?" She tugged her father's arm gently.

Mr. Mouseling set down his newspaper. "It'll be a tight squeeze…" he said thoughtfully.

"And it's for a long time," added Mrs. Mouseling.

But Angelina was determined. "I don't mind," she insisted. "I *want* to share my room!"

Angelina's room *was* a bit crowded with two beds, but Angelina was too excited to care.

"We're going to have the best summer ever," she said when Anya finally arrived. "We'll share everything!"

Angelina tucked Anya's books beside her own on the windowsill. She cleared some space on the nightstand for Anya's picture of her parents. And she pulled a pink tutu out of her closet for Anya to wear to ballet class.

"Thanks, Angelina," said Anya, "but I've never done ballet before. What if I don't fit in?"

Angelina put an arm around her new friend. "Don't worry, Anya," she said. "I'll look after you. I promise."

At ballet class the next day, Anya worked very hard to follow Angelina's steps.

"You dance so well, Anya!" exclaimed Alice when the music ended. "It's as if you've been doing ballet for ages."

When Miss Lilly asked the mouselings to choose partners to make up a special dance, Angelina was worried. Would Alice be hurt if Angelina danced with Anya? But Alice didn't mind at all, and Anya had a wonderful idea—she and Angelina would dance the story of the kingfishers.

"It's a Dacovian story," explained Anya, "about two kingfishers who are good friends and stay together their whole lives."

"How lovely!" said Miss Lilly. "A dance of friendship." She pulled the two mouselings into a warm embrace.

Angelina and Anya practiced their special dance every day at ballet class. Anya's steps had become as graceful as Angelina's.

"Anya, you are doing so well!" Miss Lilly said when the partners finished their dance.

Then Miss Lilly pulled Angelina aside. "The Dacovian Ballet is coming to the Theatre Royal again," said Miss Lilly. "I think it's a good idea for me to invite Anya this year, don't you?"

Angelina was terribly disappointed. Miss Lilly always took *her* to the Dacovian Ballet. It wasn't fair!

But "Yes, Miss Lilly" was all Angelina could say.

"Good, then," said Miss Lilly, patting Angelina's shoulder. "And tell your mother I'm looking forward to dinner tonight."

That evening, everyone fussed over the Dacovian dinner
that Anya had helped to prepare.

"I'm going to show Mrs. Mouseling how to make cheese
soufflé, too," Anya said to Miss Lilly, who sat across the
table from her.

Angelina sighed and played with her food. She wished
she could think of something else to talk about. Then she
spotted the kingfisher costumes hanging in the corner.
"What do you think of our costumes, Miss Lilly?" Angelina
asked brightly.

"They're beautiful!" said Miss Lilly. "Anya is learning ballet so fast," she said to Mrs. Mouseling. "Soon she'll apply to the Dacovian Ballet Academy!"

Anya, Anya, Anya, thought Angelina miserably. Why wouldn't everyone stop talking about Anya?

After dinner, Angelina found Anya sitting in the dark
bedroom, staring at the picture of her parents. She looked
lonely, and for a moment, Angelina felt sorry for her. Then
Angelina realized *where* Anya was sitting.

"That's my bed!" Angelina snapped.

Anya jumped off the bed in surprise. "Oh!" she said.
"But I thought we were sharing everything."

"I'm not so sure now," said Angelina. Jealous, angry words tumbled out of her mouth. "I'm tired of hearing about how talented you are," Angelina cried. "And how great Dacovia is. Maybe you just should have stayed there!"

When Angelina awoke the next morning, she was feeling very sorry for the way she had acted. But when she turned to apologize to Anya, Angelina saw that Anya's bed was empty.

Angelina raced downstairs to the kitchen. "Have you seen Anya?" Angelina asked her mother desperately.

"No," said Mrs. Mouseling. "Isn't she in your room?"

Angelina rushed out the front door without answering, but the sound of the ringing telephone called her back.

"Oh, hello, Miss Lilly," said Mrs. Mouseling into the receiver. "Anya's at your house? Good gracious! I had no idea!"

Angelina sat, her head hung low, in Miss Lilly's parlor. She was too ashamed to look at Miss Lilly.

"I'm very disappointed in you," said Miss Lilly. "How would you like to be away from your parents for such a long time?"

"I wouldn't," Angelina answered in a small voice.
"Oh, I've been so horrid to Anya! Please may I see her and apologize?"

"Of course you may," said Miss Lilly. She disappeared down the hall, and Angelina waited nervously in the parlor.

But when Miss Lilly returned, Anya wasn't with her. "I'm sorry," said Miss Lilly gently, "but Anya doesn't wish to see you. Perhaps you can speak to her at ballet class."

Angelina's heart sank. Would Anya ever forgive her?

At ballet class, Angelina spotted Anya across the room, talking with William. Angelina took a deep breath, and then hurried over.

But Anya wasn't happy to see Angelina. "I don't want to dance with you," Anya said frostily. "I'm dancing with Alice."

After class, a very sad Angelina trudged home beside Alice. "I just wish she'd let me apologize," said Angelina.

Alice felt terrible. "I wish I could help," she said. "Anya wants to practice with me down by the river, wearing your costumes so that we'll feel like real kingfishers."

Angelina stopped in her tracks and smiled thoughtfully. Now she knew *just* how to apologize to Anya.

Angelina dressed in her kingfisher costume and hurried down to the river. Anya was already there. "Hi, Alice!" Anya called.

Angelina breathed a sigh of relief as she took her starting position. Anya didn't recognize her!

On the count of three, the mouselings began to dance across the grassy riverbank. They fluttered apart and then swooped back together, just like real kingfishers. They dipped low and rose up again, wings outstretched.

When the dance ended, Angelina pulled off her mask. "I'm sorry, Anya," she whispered anxiously, hoping Anya wouldn't be angry that she had been fooled.

Anya was silent for a moment, and then she burst into tears. "I'm sorry, too!" she cried. She threw her arms open wide, and the two friends hugged each other tightly.

Angelina and Anya sat together in a bus seat, chattering excitedly. "Wasn't the prince amazing?" said Angelina.

"Oh, yes," said Anya. "Thank you, Miss Lilly. It was the best show I've ever seen!"

Miss Lilly, who was seated behind the two mouselings, leaned forward. "And to think," she said, "that my darling Angelina believed she wasn't going to the Dacovian Ballet this year, when I had three tickets all along!"

That evening, Anya started packing her things, for tomorrow she would return home. She handed the pink tutu to Angelina.

"Oh, no," Angelina insisted. "Keep it. What's mine is yours, remember?" she said warmly, and *this* time, Angelina truly meant it.

Angelina, the Mouse Detective

From the script by Laura Beaumont

BASED ON THE CLASSIC PICTURE BOOKS
BY KATHARINE HOLABIRD AND HELEN CRAIG

On a bright, sunny morning, Alice and Henry walked together to Angelina's house. Henry tossed his favorite red ball up into the air.

"Be careful now, Henry," Alice warned as they neared Mrs. Hodgepodge's yard.

But Henry's next toss was a little too high, and the ball sprang away from him. It bounced one, two, three times before plunking down in Mrs. Hodgepodge's garden.

Mrs. Hodgepodge snatched up the ball and shook her finger at the mouselings. "How many times do I have to tell you I do *not* want balls coming into my garden!" she spat.

"We're sorry, Mrs. Hodgepodge," said Alice, and Henry bowed his head politely. But Mrs. Hodgepodge would not return the ball, and they had to continue on to Angelina's without it.

Alice and Henry met Angelina just as she was stepping through her front gate. Angelina's nose was buried in a book.

"Oh, Angelina!" exclaimed Alice, rushing to her friend's side. "Is that the new Monty the Mouse Detective book?"

"Yes!" said Angelina. "It's 'The Case of the Missing Cheese.' Monty is just about to open the cupboard door…"

"What happens next?" asked Henry, his eyes wide.

Angelina read to her friends as they walked down the lane. "Monty reaches out to turn the handle," Angelina continued. "The door swings open, and the cheese is gone! He says—"

"Hey, what's going on over there?" interrupted Alice, pointing toward Miss Lilly's yard. Miss Lilly and Mrs. Thimble stood talking with Inspector Scrabble, who was scratching notes onto a pad of paper.

"Yours is the third garden gnome that has been stolen this week, Miss Lilly," said the inspector. "But I'm afraid there's not much I can do."

Henry sighed. "If only Monty the Mouse Detective were here," he said.

"Yes," said Angelina thoughtfully. "If only…" Suddenly, she had an idea.

Later that day, three mouselings popped up from behind
Miss Lilly's hedge. Angelina wore a cap pulled low over her eyes,
and Henry peered through a very large magnifying glass.

"So, what do we do first?" asked Alice.

"We dust for paw prints," said Angelina, Mouse Detective. "Let's check the gate."

But the only paw prints on the gate belonged to Henry, who had discovered that the gate was the perfect place to practice gymnastics.

"Now what?" asked Alice.

Angelina consulted her Mouse Detective book. "Monty would look for clues," she said. "But you need a specially trained eye. Only the most experienced investigators can find clues."

"Look what I found!" piped up Henry. He held out a floppy green garden glove.

"Henry, you're a genius!" exclaimed Angelina. "This is exactly what a gnome thief would use." She raised the glove into the air, where it was instantly plucked from her grasp.

"My gardening glove!" said Miss Lilly, dropping the glove into her shopping basket. "I've been looking for it everywhere."

Angelina sighed. She whispered to Alice, "Being a detective is *not* an easy job."

Angelina flipped through the pages of her Mouse Detective book. "I know," she said thoughtfully. "Suspects! Monty would find suspects."

"What does a suspect look like?" asked Henry, searching the ground with his magnifying glass.

"Like that, Henry," whispered Alice. She nodded toward the lane. Captain Millar crept alongside a hedge, carrying a large sack. He peered over the tops of the bushes, as if looking for something on the ground below.

"Follow him!" Angelina cried. The mouselings tracked Captain Millar around the bend to Mrs. Chalk's backyard, where a large bonfire burned. Captain Millar set down the sack and joined Mrs. Chalk and Mrs. Pinkpaws around the fire.

Angelina sprang into action. She grabbed the sack and hoisted it into the air. "You thought you could get away with it, eh?" she declared. "You know, it's really not nice to go around taking people's…"—she dumped the contents of the sack onto the ground—"mushrooms?"

A pile of red-capped mushrooms spilled from the bag. Angelina gulped. Captain Millar hadn't been stealing gnomes at all. He had been ridding gardens of poisonous old toadstools.

93

That evening, a very discouraged Angelina walked home alone.
Night was falling, and everything seemed bleak and gloomy.
Angelina had done her best to find the thief, but the gnomes were
still missing.

As Angelina passed Mrs. Hodgepodge's gate, something caught
her eye. A light burned in the garden shed. Through the window,
Angelina could see a shadowy figure holding what appeared to be…

"A garden gnome!" Angelina exclaimed. "Oh, what would Monty do now?" She took a shaky breath and crept through the gate. She bent low beneath the window of the shed and flung open the door. There, holding a gnome, was Mrs. Hodgepodge!

Mrs. Hodgepodge's hands flew into the air, and the gnome fell to the floor with a *crash!*

"Mrs. Hodgepodge!" cried Angelina. "You're the gnome thief?"

Mrs. Hodgepodge closed the door quickly behind Angelina. "I wasn't stealing the gnomes," Mrs. Hodgepodge insisted. "Just smartening them up." She showed Angelina a gnome that had been freshly painted.

"Oh, that's so nice!" Angelina said with surprise. "I can't wait to tell everybody."

Mrs. Hodgepodge looked horrified. "Don't you dare!" she said. "I can't have people thinking I'm a nice old lady. They'd all be coming around for tea," she added with a wink.

The next morning, Alice and Henry joined Angelina to hear the end of "The Case of the Missing Cheese." Henry brought a brand-new blue ball, which he kept a very close eye on.

Angelina read slowly so that her friends could savor every word. "Monty knows that whoever stole the cheese will return to the scene of the crime," she said. "And standing there, holding a large packet of cheese biscuits, is the thief! Monty said—"

"Hey!" Alice interrupted. "What's going on over there?"

Once again, Inspector Scrabble stood beside Miss Lilly's garden gate. The inspector, Miss Lilly, and Mrs. Thimble all seemed to be staring at something in the corner of the yard.

Angelina and her friends raced to the gate and peered over the top. There, nestled beside a hedge, was Miss Lilly's garden gnome.

"It's the strangest thing I've ever seen," announced the inspector. "All the gnomes have been fixed up and returned to their owners!"

"Well, that case is closed, but what about the case of the missing cheese?" asked Alice as the mouselings continued on their way. Henry happily bounced his ball beside Alice.

Angelina turned to the last page of her book. "It was Mr. Churn, the cheesemaker!"

"But he seemed so nice!" said Alice. Just then, Henry's ball bounced off a tree and into Mrs. Hodgepodge's yard. The mouselings held their breath, waiting for Mrs. Hodgepodge to scold them. Instead, she tossed the ball right back over the gate to Henry.

"You see, Alice?" said Angelina. "People aren't always what they seem." She giggled and winked at Mrs. Hodgepodge, who winked back before returning to her garden shed.

The Rose Fairy Princess

From the script by Barbara Slade

BASED ON THE CLASSIC PICTURE BOOKS
BY KATHARINE HOLABIRD AND HELEN CRAIG

"And again, Angelina!" called Miss Lilly.

Angelina danced onto the stage. This was her last chance
to prove that she would make the very best Rose Fairy
Princess in the exciting new ballet.

Angelina twirled and leaped gracefully across the floor. She was concentrating so hard on dancing that she didn't notice that the ribbon of one of her slippers had come undone! As Angelina began her final leap, she tripped on the ribbon and toppled over with a *thud*.

"Never mind, Angelina," giggled Priscilla Pinkpaws as she walked by with her twin sister, Penelope.

"After all," added Penelope, "you can always join the chorus of dancing flowers!"

Later that day, all the little ballerinas crowded around
Miss Lilly to hear the results of the audition.

Miss Lilly raised her clipboard in the air and said,
"The Rose Fairy Princess shall be danced by—"

"Oh, Miss Lilly!" Penelope interrupted. "I knew I'd get the part. I just knew it!"

"Penelope, darling," said Miss Lilly gently, "I am sorry, but this time, Angelina will dance the part of the Rose Fairy Princess. And you, Penelope, will make a beautiful dancing flower."

Angelina gasped, "You mean…I got the part?" She could hardly believe it was true!

As Angelina and Alice left the dressing room that afternoon, Angelina chattered excitedly. "Oh, Alice, I got the part! I'm going to practice every day. I'm going to be the *best* Rose Fairy Princess—ever!"

Angelina twirled all the way down the long hall and found Miss Lilly talking to the stage manager.

"A single wire!" exclaimed Miss Lilly. "What a perfect finale. My beautiful Rose Fairy Princess will fly across the stage on a single wire!" Then she noticed Angelina. "It's marvelous, don't you think, Angelina?"

But Angelina's stomach was doing flip-flops. "A single wire?" she whispered to herself. "Oh, no!"

"Miss Lilly?" Angelina began timidly. She held her tail to keep it from quivering. "I was just wondering if a single wire is such a good idea. The audience might see the wire, and…um…that could be a-a-a very big problem."

"A problem?" said Miss Lilly, holding up a beautiful pink tutu with wings.

"Yes! But a ladder…," Angelina continued hopefully, "a tall ladder decorated with vines to look like a tower—that would be something!"

Miss Lilly didn't seem to be listening. She held the tutu in front of Angelina to check its size, then lifted the winged tutu into the air and said, "Oh, Angelina, just imagine the feeling of soaring above the stage like a bird. You will be magnificent!"

But Angelina wasn't so sure.

"Why, you're the bravest, most daring mouse I've ever known," said Alice, trying to comfort Angelina.

"But this is just one little wire!" Angelina exclaimed. "What if it breaks?"

"It won't break," Alice reassured her. "I'm sure that Miss Lilly…"

But something had caught Angelina's eye—a poster for the circus, featuring Zivo, the magnificent acrobat. He would be able to help!

Soon the mouselings were peeking through the flaps
of a colorful circus tent. "There he is!" said Angelina.
"The most daring trapeze artist in the world." Angelina
grabbed Alice's paw and pulled her into the tent.

"Mr. Zivo!" Angelina called, craning her neck to watch him as he sailed through the air on a trapeze. "Can you teach me to fly on a single wire?"

Zivo released his grip on the trapeze, did a magnificent triple flip, and landed on the ground beside Angelina.

"A single wire?" he asked. "Little mouseling, you've come to the right place. Follow me!" He led Angelina toward the huge ladder in the center of the ring.

Angelina climbed the ladder, which seemed to stretch
on forever. Finally she stepped onto a tiny platform near
the top of the tent. She strapped on a harness and then
reached out to touch the hook that Zivo had lowered for
her. The hook felt shaky and fragile.

"Oh," Angelina whimpered. "I can't do it." She suddenly
felt dizzy. Before she could fasten the hook to her harness,
Angelina lost her balance and fell down, down, down…
Plunk! She bounced three times before settling into a
tangled heap in the middle of the safety net.

Alice had been watching from the stands, and she rushed to the net. "Oh, Angelina," Alice said kindly. "Maybe it's not so bad being a dancing flower after all."

That afternoon at rehearsal, Angelina danced her part
nervously, dreading the moment when she would have to
face the single wire. Then, she had an idea. She clasped
her hand against her forehead and swayed across the stage.
She spun around once and landed on the floor in a faint.

"Angelina," Miss Lilly said gently, "are you alright?"

"Oh, dear," Angelina said in her weakest voice. "I must have fainted."

"She probably won't be able to dance the part, Miss Lilly!" Penelope piped up from the circle of dancers. "But I can! I know every step!"

"Thank you, Penelope," said Miss Lilly as she helped Angelina sit up. "But I'm sure Angelina will be alright. My little Rose Fairy Princess just needs her rest."

On the evening of the performance, Alice handed Angelina
a small gift.

"It's for good luck," Alice said. "I mean, not that you'll
need it," she added quickly.

Angelina opened the box and found a delicate little bird attached to a thin wire. She smiled as she watched the bird swing back and forth on the wire. But then—*snap!* The wire broke!

"Oh, Alice," Angelina said. "What am I going to do?"

"I don't know," replied Alice. "I wish I could do something. I'd even fly across the stage for you if I could."

Angelina threw her arms around Alice. "That's it!" she cried. "You'll fly across the stage instead of me. We'll switch costumes right before the finale, and no one will ever know!"

In front of a large audience that evening, Angelina danced the part of the Rose Fairy Princess beautifully. As the grand finale approached, she disappeared behind the scenery and motioned to Alice, who was still dancing onstage. "Now, Alice!" Angelina whispered urgently.

Alice tiptoed away from the line of dancing flowers and made her way toward Angelina in the dim light backstage.

"I'm coming, Angelina!" she called. But then her costume snagged on a nail at the back of the Rose Fairy castle. Alice struggled furiously, trying to free herself, but it was no use!

The applause ended and the music for the next scene
began. "Alice?" Angelina called into the darkness. Where
was her friend?

As the curtains parted, Angelina knew what she had to do.
She took a deep breath. "I won't let you down, Miss Lilly,"
she said, slipping her arms into the harness. "After all, I am
the Rose Fairy Princess!"

As she was lifted into the air, Angelina's fear gave way to
excitement, and then pure joy! She soared through the air,
high above the dancing flowers. The audience leaped to
their feet and applauded. Angelina felt magnificent, just as
Miss Lilly had said she would.

The next day, Angelina hung her little bird in her bedroom window.

"You were a wonderful dancing flower," she said to Alice, who was mending her torn costume.

"Do you really think so?" Alice asked, beaming.

"Yes," said Angelina. "And you know what? I'm going to talk to Miss Lilly about doing a ballet about a circus girl." Angelina gave the little bird a gentle push. "A dancing circus girl who flies across the stage on a single wire!" she added.

"But, Angelina…" Alice said in a worried voice.

"I'll play the circus girl," Angelina continued. "And it will be the best ballet ever!"

Angelina's Lucky Penny

From the script by James Mason

BASED ON THE CLASSIC PICTURE BOOKS
BY KATHARINE HOLABIRD AND HELEN CRAIG

"The Swan Princess! The Swan Princess!" Angelina and her best friend, Alice, sang together as they skipped down the path to ballet class.

"The best movie ever! And this afternoon, *we* get to see it," Angelina exclaimed. She couldn't believe their good luck.

Angelina skipped on, but Alice called to her, "Angelina, wait! Where's your ribbon?"

Angelina checked her head. "I had it on when we left home," she said. She searched the ground all around, but there was no sign of the ribbon. She would have to go to ballet class without it.

"Now you, Angelina," said Miss Lilly. Her students were practicing their steps for the big audition the next day.

Angelina leaped into the air, twirled around in a circle, and landed. But, oops! She wobbled a bit on her toes as she finished.

"Darling!" said Miss Lilly. "Think about those steps. You must be absolutely still after you've landed."

Angelina's face fell. She had tried so hard to keep still, but it was difficult. Would she ever get it right?

Angelina watched unhappily as Priscilla Pinkpaws took her turn and landed perfectly.

"Beautiful, darling!" chimed Miss Lilly. "You see, Angelina, that is how you must do it!"

Angelina tried to push away all her bad feelings. She would just have to work harder, she decided.

"Come on, Angelina, or we'll be late for the movie," said Alice after class.

"I'm sorry," Angelina said firmly, "but I can't go to the movie. I've got to go home and practice my dance routine."

Alice walked Angelina part of the way home. They played leapfrog along the path. As Angelina sprang over Alice's shoulders, she felt her bag slip off her arm. The bag slid along the ground and stopped just short of a puddle.

When Angelina bent down to pick up the bag, she noticed a coin lying in the puddle.

"Hey, it's a lucky penny! It stopped your bag from getting wet," said Alice excitedly.

And then Angelina spotted something else. "You're right, it *is* a lucky penny. Look what I found!" she said, lifting her hair ribbon from the tall grass beside the path. She tied the ribbon on her head and said, "Hurry up, Alice! We're going to be late for the movie, and we still have to get Henry."

"But, Angelina, don't you need to go home and practice?" asked Alice.

Angelina shook her head. "I've got a lucky penny. I don't need to practice!" she said as she raced off down the path.

Angelina, Alice, and Henry searched for three empty seats in the village hall. As they sat down, Henry turned to Angelina and whispered, "Please, can I see it now, Angelina?"

Angelina handed the lucky penny to her little cousin.
"Be careful, Henry. It's very special," she said. She turned
the coin over and showed him the date. "See? That's the
year I was born!"

"Oh!" gasped Henry.

When the lights dimmed, Angelina hastily dropped the
penny back into her bag. She was so excited about the
movie that she didn't notice that the penny missed the bag.
It bounced on the floor and rolled away into the darkness.

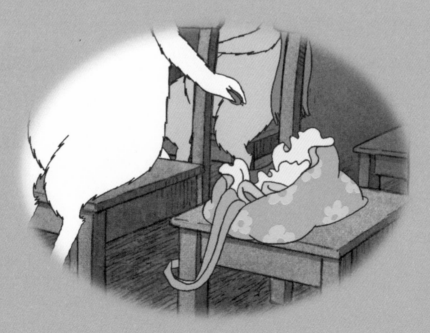

"Priscilla Pinkpaws will be so disappointed when I get the part," said Angelina as the mouselings walked home after the movie. "Watch this!" She sprang along the path, spun around in the air, and toppled suddenly to the ground.

"Wha-what happened?" Angelina stammered. "Where's the penny?"

"I'm sure it's in your bag," said Alice. But it was *not*. Angelina dumped her things onto the ground, and Alice and Henry helped her sort through them. The penny wasn't there.

Angelina's heart sank. "It's gone," she sighed. "No wonder I can't do the steps. We've *got* to find that penny!"

The mouselings rushed back to the village hall. The doors were locked, but Angelina saw that two wooden planks in the back door were loose. She pushed the planks apart and tried to squeeze through the gap, but she was too big.

"Will you try, Henry?" she pleaded with her cousin, who was the only one small enough to fit.

Henry peered through the gap. He didn't like the dark, but he wanted to be brave for Angelina. "Al-alright," he squeaked as he squeezed his little body through the crack.

"Just look for anything round and shiny," Angelina called after him.

A moment later, Henry popped back out. He proudly
dumped an assortment of shiny round objects on the
ground.

"Well done, Henry!" Angelina praised him as she and Alice
began sifting through the objects. But there was no penny.

"I'm sorry," Henry said in a tiny voice as he walked home beside Angelina.

"It's not your fault, Henry," said Angelina. She took Henry's paw and gave it a squeeze.

"Shouldn't you be at home practicing, Angelina?" a voice called from down the street. Priscilla and her twin sister, Penelope, were sitting on a low stone wall.

Angelina tried to ignore them, but Henry said boldly, "She doesn't need to practice, 'cause she found a lucky penny!"

The twins fell into a fit of laughter. "A lucky penny!" howled Penelope. "There's no such thing."

Priscilla jumped off the wall and began to twirl. "Besides," she said, "I don't need luck. I'm the best dancer!"

Angelina knew that Priscilla *was* a good dancer. And now that the lucky penny was gone, Angelina would have to work very hard to earn the part.

Angelina practiced her ballet steps late into the evening. Again and again, she leaped across her room, spun into the air, and landed in front of her mirror.

"I've nearly got it!" Angelina said aloud after landing firmly on her toes. But she returned to her starting position and practiced the steps again. They had to be perfect!

When Angelina and Alice arrived at Miss Lilly's Ballet
School the next morning, Henry was waiting for them.
"This is for you, Angelina!" he said proudly, holding out
his paw. "It's your lucky penny."

Angelina grasped the penny and checked the date. "Well,
Henry, you clever thing!" she exclaimed.

Priscilla watched them from across the room. She made a
face at Angelina, but Angelina just smiled back at her.

"Take your places, darlings!" called Miss Lilly.

Priscilla's audition was first, and she performed the steps perfectly. When she was finished, she stepped back into line, very pleased with herself.

"And now, Angelina, it's your turn," announced Miss Lilly.

Angelina took a deep breath and stepped forward. She
let the music carry her across the dance floor. She leaped
gracefully into the air, twirled around, and landed steadily
on one slipper, her eyes closed and her arms stretched
upward.

As Angelina waited nervously, Miss Lilly and a lady from
the Theater Royal spoke together in hushed voices. They
reviewed Miss Lilly's notes and then smiled at each other.
Miss Lilly nodded her head.

"Now, my darlings," she said dramatically, "the results.
Angelina will dance the part!"

The mouselings gathered at Henry's house after the
auditions. Angelina spun Henry around and hugged
him tightly.

"Oh, Henry!" she exclaimed. "Thanks to you, I got the
part! But where on earth did you find my penny?"

Henry untangled himself from Angelina's arms and reached under the bed. He pulled out a glass jar full of pennies. "I've got lots of lucky pennies!" he announced.

Angelina and Alice looked at each other with wide eyes, and then giggled. Angelina knelt beside Henry and held out the penny he had given her. "Will you look after this for me, Henry?" she asked.

"Okay!" said Henry brightly. He dropped the penny into his jar and said, "I'm going to be very lucky, aren't I?"

"You *are*, Henry," Angelina said tenderly. "You are."